Saving the Pond

Story by Diana Noonan
Illustrations by Dori Berkovic

Contents

Chapter 1

A Little Pond

George and Evie moved to a new house with their dad and their big sister, Claire.

In front of the house was a rose garden. Behind the house, George and Evie found a little pond.

Every afternoon,
George and Evie went down to the pond.

If they kept very quiet,
they could see frogs and insects everywhere!

Chapter 2

Dad's Apple Trees

One day, Dad came home with four apple trees.

"I'm going to plant these apple trees behind the house," he said.

Dad started to dig some holes for the trees.
But the ground was too wet and muddy,
and the holes filled up with water.

"I'll soon get this place dry," said Dad. "I'll move all the water and mud away with my shovel."

"But Dad! What about the pond?" said the children together.

"We can't have apple trees *and* a pond," said Dad. "The pond will have to go."

Chapter 3

A Plan to Save the Pond

George and Evie quickly made a plan to save the pond.

"Can we please take some photos with your phone?" Evie asked Claire.

"Yes, you can," said Claire.

That afternoon,
George and Evie hid behind some long grass,
near the pond.

Soon, they saw some frogs
and insects.

Evie carefully held up Claire's phone
and took a photo.

It started to get dark,
but the children stayed hidden
behind the long grass.

Evie took some more photos
of the frogs and insects.

That night, George and Evie made an e-book with their photos.
They called it *Why We Love Our Pond.*

In the morning,
the children showed the e-book to Dad.

"I can see why you want the pond to stay,"
said Dad.
"But where can I put my apple trees?"

"You could plant them in the *front* garden," said George.

"Yes!" shouted Evie.
"They will look great beside the roses."

Chapter 4

Dad's Surprise

The next morning,
George and Evie helped Dad
plant his apple trees in the front garden.

In the afternoon,
Dad went into the garage.
He took some bits of wood with him.

"What are you making?" asked George.

"It's a surprise!" said Dad.

He was in the garage for a long time.

The next day, George and Evie found a little chair beside the pond.

"I love my apple trees," said Dad.

"And we love our pond!" said the children.